Shortcut

Shortcut

David Macaulay

Houghton Mifflin Company Boston

1995

To Mom and Dad, who began their journey together fifty years ago. Love and thanks.

Copyright © 1995 by David Macaulay

Library of Congress Cataloging-in-Publication Data

Macaulay, David.
   Shortcut / by David Macaulay.
   p.   cm.
   Summary: Visual clues provide answers to the mysterious
interrelationship of a series of brief stories.
   ISBN 0-395-52436-9
   [1. Literary recreations.]   I. Title.
PZ7.M1197Sh   1995   95-2542
[Fic]—dc20   CIP
                           AC

Printed in the United States of America
BVG 10 9 8 7 6 5 4 3 2 1
Walter Lorraine Books

CHAPTER ONE

Albert and June are up early. It is market day.

Once a week they take their ripest melons into town.
As they cross the bridge, Albert and June always make a wish.

To save time, they will take the shortcut.
Albert removes his coat and helps June up the hill.

When they reach the top, Albert gets his coat and they are off again.
In a little while they stop to eat at the Railway Café.

June is very hungry. She stretches to reach some tasty clover.
After lunch, they continue toward town, crooning their favorite songs.

A rope blocks their path—but not for long.

Their melons are very popular, and the wagon is soon empty.
Once again, Albert and June get their wish.
They are home before dark.

CHAPTER TWO

Patty and Pearl are the best of friends.
They go almost everywhere together.

When Patty is busy, Pearl relaxes near the abandoned railway line.
One day, Pearl disappears without a trace. Almost.

CHAPTER THREE

With his balloon firmly tied, Professor Tweet spends his days
studying bird behavior.

Suddenly the balloon breaks free.

It is heading straight for the cathedral town of Fauxville.

Thinking quickly, the professor tosses everything
over the side. The balloon starts to rise.

And just in time. Tweet and his balloon are safe.

CHAPTER FOUR

Someone has opened the switch, sending
the Darlington Cannonball onto the abandoned line.

It soon picks up an extra passenger and disappears into a tunnel.

After crossing Chestnut Street and the old trestle,
the train rolls on toward the end of the line.

CHAPTER FIVE

Sybil is off to market.

She races through town and country.

Though she follows the sign, it is still a long, long way.
By the time she arrives, Albert is out of melons and she is out of luck.

Shortcut

Long Long Way

CHAPTER SIX

Patty must find her best friend. First she tries all the familiar places.

Having no luck, she takes to the road.

Patty searches high and low.
In the end, there is only one place left to look.

CHAPTER SEVEN

Bob sleeps all day. He loves the peace and quiet of the river.
In his favorite dream, he is the admiral of the fleet.

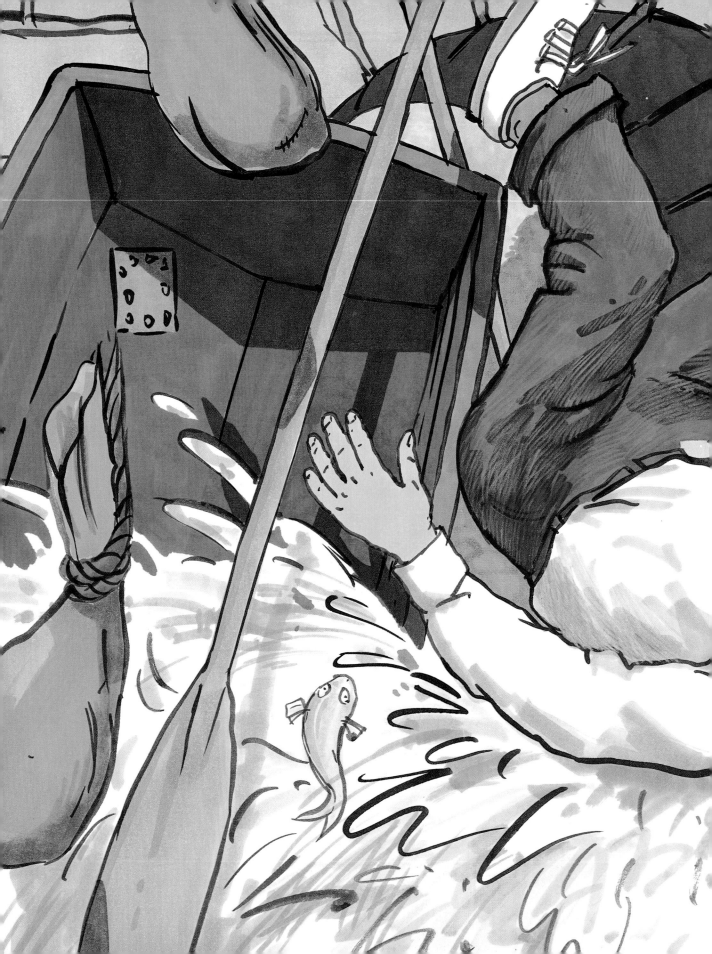

Suddenly he is thrown from his boat. Fortunately, he sinks
to the bottom, which is how he makes his dream come true.

CHAPTER EIGHT

Professor Tweet has lost his balloon forever.

But by rescuing Clarinda's crafty cockatoo, he has captured
her heart and happily takes up safer work.

CHAPTER NINE

Even without tracks, the train keeps moving.

It finally comes to rest at the beach.
This is not on the schedule.

EPILOGUE

A muffled snort tells Patty where to dig. When Pearl recovers
from her adventure, the two go almost everywhere together.
But never by train.